# Collins English Library
## Series editors: K R Cripwell and Lewis Jones

A library of graded
native readers. Th
idiom and sentenc
in *A Teacher's Gui*
level. Level 1 has a
words, 3: 1000 wor
which are asteriske

**Level One**

Inspector Holt: Where is Bill Ojo? *John Tully*
Crocodile! *K R Cripwell*
Four Short Stories* *Margery Morris*
Fast Money *K R Cripwell*
It's a Trick! *Lewis Jones*
The Story of Macbeth *from Shakespeare*
Tin Lizzie* *Jane Homeshaw*
Dead in the Morning* *Jane Homeshaw*
Letters from the Dead* *Jane Homeshaw*
Taxi! *Jane Homeshaw*
The Pathfinders* *Jane Homeshaw*
Inspector Holt: Cats in the Dark* *John Tully*
Inspector Holt and the Chinese Necklace *John Tully*
Journey to Universe City *Leslie Dunkling*
Three Folk Tales* *Margaret Naudi*
The Man with Three Fingers *John Tully*
Fastline UK *Jane Homeshaw*
The Grey Rider *Steve Rabley*
Love Me Tomorrow *Jane Homeshaw*

**Level Two**

The Magic Garden *K R Cripwell*
Muhammed Ali: King of the Ring *John Tully*
Inspector Holt Gets His Man* *John Tully*
The Canterville Ghost* *Oscar Wilde*
The Prince and the Poor Boy *Mark Twain*
Inspector Holt: The Bridge* *John Tully*
Oliver Twist *Charles Dickens*
Two Roman Stories *from Shakespeare*
The Titanic is Sinking* *K R Cripwell*
The Wrestler *K R Cripwell*
Madame Tussaud's* *Lewis Jones*
Three Sherlock Holmes Adventures* *A Conan Doyle*
The Story of Scotland Yard *Lewis Jones*
The Charlie Chaplin Story* *Jane Homeshaw*
Charles and Diana *Margery Morris*
A King's Love Story *K R Cripwell*
Dangerous Earth *Jane Homeshaw*
Chariots of Fire* *W J Weatherby*
Shark Attack *Jan Keane*
The Complete Robot: Selected Stories *Isaac Asimov*
Roadie *Chris Banks*
The Mystery of Dr Fu Manchu *Sax Rohmer*

**Level Three**

Climb a Lonely Hill *Lilith Norman*
Custer's Gold *Kenneth Ulyatt*
Gunshot Grand Prix *Douglas Rutherford*
David Copperfield* *Charles Dickens*
Born Free *Joy Adamson*

Five Ghost Stories* *Viola Huggins*
Three English Kings *from Shakespeare*
An American Tragedy *Theodore Dreiser*
Six American Stories* *N Wymer*
Emma and I *Sheila Hocken*
Little Women *Louisa M Alcott*
The Picture of Dorian Gray* *Oscar Wilde*
Maimunah *David Hill*
Marilyn Monroe *Peter Dainty*
Bruce Springsteen *Toni Murphy*
Is That It? *Bob Geldof*
Short Stories *Oscar Wilde*
A Room with a View *E M Forster*
The Importance of Being Ernest *Oscar Wilde*
The Lost World *Sir Arthur Conan Doyle*
Arab Folk Tales *Helen Thomson*
Computers: From Beads to Bytes *Peter Dewar*

**Level Four**

The White South *Hammond Innes*
A Christmas Carol *Charles Dickens*
King Solomon's Mines* *H Rider Haggard*
Jane Eyre *Charlotte Brontë*
Pride and Prejudice *Jane Austen*
Dr Jekyll and Mr Hyde* *R L Stevenson*
Huckleberry Finn *Mark Twain*
Landslide *Desmond Bagley*
Nothing is the Number When You Die *Joan Fleming*
The African Child *Camara Laye*
The Lovely Lady and other Stories *D H Lawrence*
Airport International *Brian Moynahan*
The Secret Sharer and other Sea Stories *Joseph Conrad*
Death in Vienna? *K E Rowlands*
Hostage Tower* *Alistair MacLean*
The Potter's Wheel *Chukwuemeka Ike*
Tina Turner *Stephen Rabley*
Campbell's Kingdom *Hammond Innes*

**Level Five**

The Guns of Navarone *Alistair MacLean*
Geordie *David Walker*
Wuthering Heights *Emily Brontë*
Where Eagles Dare *Alistair MacLean*
Wreck of the Mary Deare *Hammond Innes*
I Know My Love *Catherine Gaskin*
Among the Elephants *Iain and Oria Douglas-Hamilton*
The Mayor of Casterbridge *Thomas Hardy*
Sense and Sensibility *Jane Austen*
The Eagle has Landed *Jack Higgins*
Middlemarch *George Eliot*
Victory *Joseph Conrad*
Experiences of Terror* *Roland John*
Japan: Islands in the Mist *Peter Milward*

**Level Six**

Doctor Zhivago *Boris Pasternak*
The Glory Boys *Gerald Seymour*
In the Shadow of Man *Jane Goodall*
Harry's Game *Gerald Seymour*
House of a Thousand Lanterns *Victoria Holt*
Hard Times *Charles Dickens*
Sons and Lovers *D H Lawrence*
The Dark Frontier *Eric Ambler*
Vanity Fair *William Thackeray*
Inspector Ghote Breaks an Egg *H R F Keating*

Collins English Library Level 3

# ARAB
# FOLK
# TALES

Abridged and simplified
by Helen Thomson

© Collins 1989

Printed and published in Great Britain by
William Collins Sons and Co Ltd
Glasgow G4 0NB

All rights reserved. No part of this book
may be reproduced, stored in a retrieval
system, or transmitted in any form or by
any means, electronic, mechanical, photocopying,
recording or otherwise, without the prior permission
of the Publisher.

First published in Collins English Library, 1989
Reprinted: 1990

ISBN 0 00 370282 0

Cover illustration by Liz Thomas
Illustrations by Sue Tong

**Contents**

| | |
|---|---|
| The Jewel in the Sand | 7 |
| Flowerlips | 14 |
| The Little Red Fish and the Shoe of Gold | 24 |
| Si Djeha Cheats the Thieves | 34 |
| God will Help | 42 |
| How Si Djeha Found a Good Meal | 48 |
| How the Animals Kept the Lions Away | 52 |
| The Farmer Without a Brain | 56 |
| A Crossword | 60 |

# *The Jewel in the Sand*

One day Sheik Hamed was riding home with Ali, his sister's son. It was a long journey so, to pass the time, he began to tell a story. The Sheik told interesting stories so Ali enjoyed listening.

In the middle of the story something caught Ali's eye. He noticed a jewel lying on the ground. He didn't want to stop his uncle's story so he didn't say anything. Instead he let his sword down so that the point was touching the ground. As the two men rode, Ali's sword marked their way back to the camp.

When they arrived home, the Sheik went to his tent to rest. But Ali didn't go to his; he got back on his camel and followed the mark of the sword back through the dusty desert. The mark led him to the jewel.

He got off his camel and picked up the jewel. He brushed off the sand. It was a ring. "It's the most beautiful ring I have ever seen," he thought. "I can't wait to show my uncle."

Ali hurried back to the camp. He quickly went to his uncle's tent and gave him the ring. When Sheik

8

Hamed saw the lovely jewel, his heart sang with happiness.

"Who can be the owner of such a fine ring? She can only be a prince's daughter. I must find her," he said.

He called for his aunt. He told her to visit all the camps nearby. He told her to find the owner of the ring.

The old woman began her journey. She travelled from camp to camp but with no success. She didn't find the owner of the ring.

At last, after many days, she arrived at a large camp full of black tents. She entered the largest tent and was welcomed by a beautiful young woman. Her face shone as bright as the full moon. Her eyes were like lakes of deep, clear water. Her mouth was like a soft pink flower after the rains.

"Welcome old woman. May your news be good news," said the girl.

Ali's aunt rested for a while and then told her story. She showed the ring to the girl.

"Yes," said the young woman, "It is my jewel. Look." She put her hand into her pocket and pulled out a second ring. The two rings were the same.

"Now I have found you," said the old woman. "Take your jewel but first tell me your name."

"I am Asila, Prince Abdullah's daughter. But you keep the jewel and take the other as well. They are a pair. They should stay together."

When the old lady returned with the two rings the

Sheik's heart was filled with fire.

"This girl has the jewels of a prince's daughter and the kindness of a prince. What a wonderful wife she would be," he thought.

Then he called for his seven best freinds. The men got on their horses and rode to Prince Abdullah's camp. When they arrived many men came running out in welcome. Twenty camels were killed and the women cooked many tasty foods.

Sheik Hamed and his men stayed at Prince Abdullah's camp for three days and three nights. The prince was an amusing host and looked after his visitors well.

On the third night the prince called Sheik Hamed to his tent. Then he asked the Sheik the reason of his visit. The Sheik told him the story of the jewel. He explained that he wanted to marry the prince's daughter.

The prince's face dropped. He looked very sad. He loved his daughter very much. He didn't want her to go away. But how could he refuse such a good man? So with a heavy heart he said, "My daughter Asila is yours. You may marry her. I hope she brings you happiness."

When the prince told his daughter about the Sheik, she cried with sadness. "But father, what about my cousin Mohamed? Have you forgotten that I have promised to marry him? Mohamed is the finest man in the camp. I want to marry him. I don't want to marry another man."

"I'm sorry child," said her father, "I know you love Mohamed, but I can't refuse our visitor."

So, with a breaking heart, Asila got ready for the journey to the Sheik's camp. The prince gave her seventy camels. They carried beautiful coloured blankets, the finest carpets and many valuable jewels.

Sheik Hamed returned home with Asila and his people got ready for the marriage party. Many camels were killed, and for seven days the women cooked from sunrise to sunset.

When one hundred pots were full of food, the women stopped cooking and went to Asila's tent. They washed and brushed her long black hair until it shone like a silver stream in the sunlight. They painted her hands and feet and then dressed her in the richest green silk. All this time Asila sat in silence with a small sad smile on her face.

When everything was ready, sweet music began to play. The party was going to begin. Then Sheik Hamed called for Ali and said, "Ali, your Asila is waiting for you. She has kohl around her eyes and there are jewels in her hair."

"*My* Asila. But she is *yours*, uncle. You found her and asked for her," said Ali in surprise.

But the Sheik threw the marriage coat over Ali's back, "You found the jewel, so she is yours."

Ali's heart was filled with happiness. But as he walked towards Asila's tent, a good-looking man threw himself on the ground. He kissed Ali's feet.

"What do you want, stranger?" said Ali, "speak without fear."

Mistaking Ali for Sheik Hamed, the stranger said, "My name is Mohamed. This girl, Asila, is my

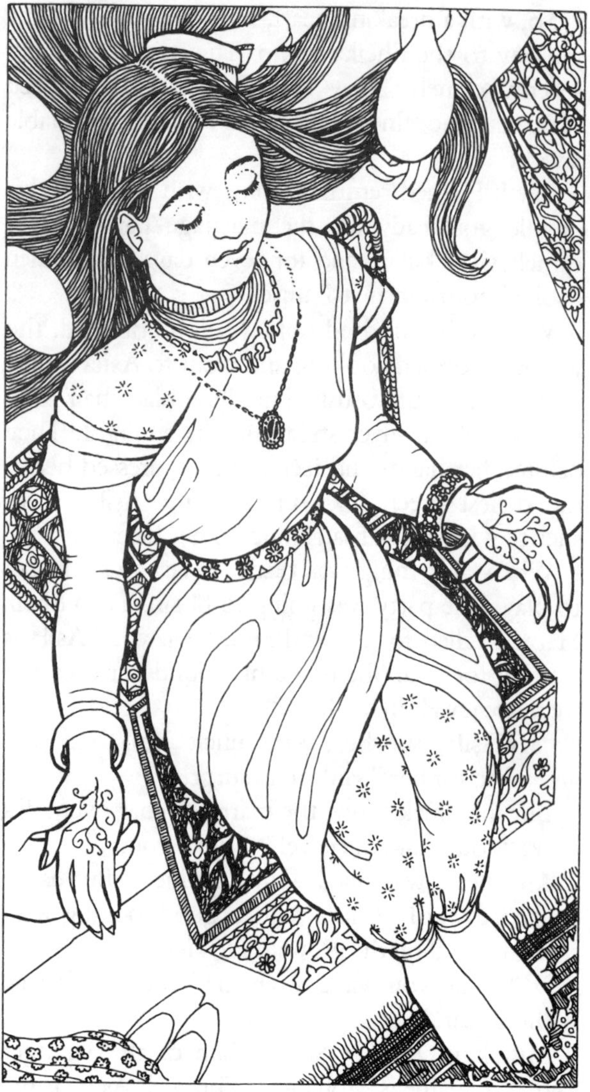

cousin. I was going to marry her. We were promised to each other."

"You ask for what is yours. May you find happiness with Asila," said Ali and threw the marriage coat over the man's back.

The next morning Sheik Hamed found Ali standing alone by his tent. Ali was wearing his old clothes.

"What are you doing here? Why aren't you with Asila?" he asked.

He listened quietly as Ali explained about Mohamed. Then he called for his eighty best camels. He put gold, jewels and his finest carpets on their backs. Then he sent the young husband and wife back to their own people.

# *Flowerlips*

There was once a successful business man who was well known in his town. Everywhere he went the people said, "Look there he is. He's the richest man in this town. His home is like the king's palace." Hearing this the rich man became very pleased with himself.

The rich man had three daughters. One morning he called for the oldest girl and said, "Why do you think I am successful?" "The answer is easy father," said the girl, "it is because you are very clever." The rich man nodded his head at this answer.

Then he called for his middle daughter and asked, "Can you explain why I am such a rich man?"

"The answer is easy father," she said, "it is because you have worked hard." The rich man smiled at this answer.

But when he questioned his youngest daughter, she said, "Your success comes from God, like all good things." This answer made her father angry and he threw the girl out of his house.

Now the girl had no home. She didn't know where to go, so she turned right and began to walk.

She walked and walked until she reached a little old house on the edge of the town. An old woman with a kind face came out of the house. She saw the sad and tired girl and felt sorry for her, so she took her inside.

The kind old lady gave the girl food and drink. The girl ate her fill and then told her story. The old lady listened and then said, "Maybe I can help you and maybe you can help me. My son needs a wife but he has no money. He is a fine man but he is poor. Will you marry him?"

The girl thought for a moment then said, "He has nothing to give and I have nowhere to live. The cooking pot has found its lid."

So the girl married the old woman's son. They lived happily together with his kind mother in the little old house.

The months passed and the young wife gave birth to a baby daughter. When the nurses lifted the baby from her mother they looked at her in wonder. "She is the loveliest child I have ever seen!" they said.

They were even more surprised when they washed her. Every drop of water she touched turned into gold! Then, when she cried, jasmines and roses fell from her lips.

The news was carried from tongue to tongue. Soon everyone was talking about this baby who turned water into gold and cried flowers. People travelled from faraway towns and cities to see her and to watch the jasmines and roses fall. She became very famous. The people called her Flowerlips.

News of the child soon reached her mother's two sisters. They soon came to visit Flowerlips. When they had seen the gold she gave her parents, they returned home biting their fingers in anger.

The years passed and Flowerlips became a beautiful young woman. Soon it was time for her to marry. Of course, many men wanted to marry her. Every day they came to ask for her hand. But her father refused all of them. Who is good enough to marry a girl that speaks flowers? No one except a king's son.

Then one day from a faraway city a prince came. He rode his camel across the desert until he reached Flowerlips' home. Her father couldn't refuse a king's son, so he agreed to let his daughter marry the prince.

The prince returned to his city a happy man. He had to get everything ready for his marriage to Flowerlips. But before he left he gave her a lovely gold ring. "Don't lose it. Keep it safe and wear it on the day of our marriage," said the prince, then he left.

Flowerlips got ready for the long journey to her new home. She was very busy. She had many things to do.

When the girl's two aunts heard of her marriage they said:

"Our sister's daughter is going to marry a prince! It is not fair."

"I must stop this wedding," thought the eldest aunt. Then an idea entered her head. She went to visit her youngest sister.

"Sister," she said to Flowerlips' mother, "my niece is too young to travel alone. It would be dangerous for her. My daughter and I will go too and take care of her." Flowerlips' mother was worried about her daughter so she happily agreed to this. "Who better to look after my daughter than her own aunt and cousin," she thought.

When everything was ready, the marriage party began the long, hot journey across the dusty desert. They travelled for many days until they were far from any town. Flowerlips grew thirsty and asked for water. But her aunt said, "If you drink, there will not be enough for us."

The girl's tongue became as dry as sand. She cried and asked her aunt again, "Please give me water."

Her aunt answered, "I'll give you water, but first you must give me your right eye."

What could the girl do? She was very thirsty. "If I don't drink I will die," she thought. So she let her aunt cut out her right eye.

Another long day passed and the girl became thirsty again. She asked her aunt for water, but her aunt said, "I'll give you water but first you must give me your left eye."

The girl's mouth was as dry as a stone so she let her aunt cut out the other eye too. Then her aunt said, "Now you have no eyes, so you can't marry the prince. My own daughter Zara will be his wife instead."

She threw Flowerlips off her camel. Then she helped her own daughter onto the camel and left Flowerlips on the dusty ground. Poor Flowerlips was too weak to move. Hungry, thirsty and unable to see she lay dying in the hot midday sun.

Then, by chance, an old man with white hair came past. His heart was moved with sadness when he saw Flowerlips. He lifted her up and led her to his home.

When the old man's family saw the girl they threw their arms in the air, "Oh grandfather, why have you brought another mouth to feed?" they cried, "we haven't even enough food for ourselves."

But the kind old man took Flowerlips into the house and gave her food and drink. Then Flowerlips asked for some water to wash herself with. When the women of the house saw the sweet flowers fall, they hurried to catch them. Then they stared in wonder as every drop of water Flowerlips touched turned into gold. Happily, they kissed Flowerlips for now they were rich. All their troubles were over.

While Flowerlips was living with the poor man's family, her aunt continued her journey with her daughter, Zara. After many days they reached the prince's city. They were warmly welcomed. Horsemen rode out to meet them and, as they walked through the streets to the palace, sweet music was played.

The prince was very pleased to see his new wife arrive safely. But when at last Zara spoke to him, he

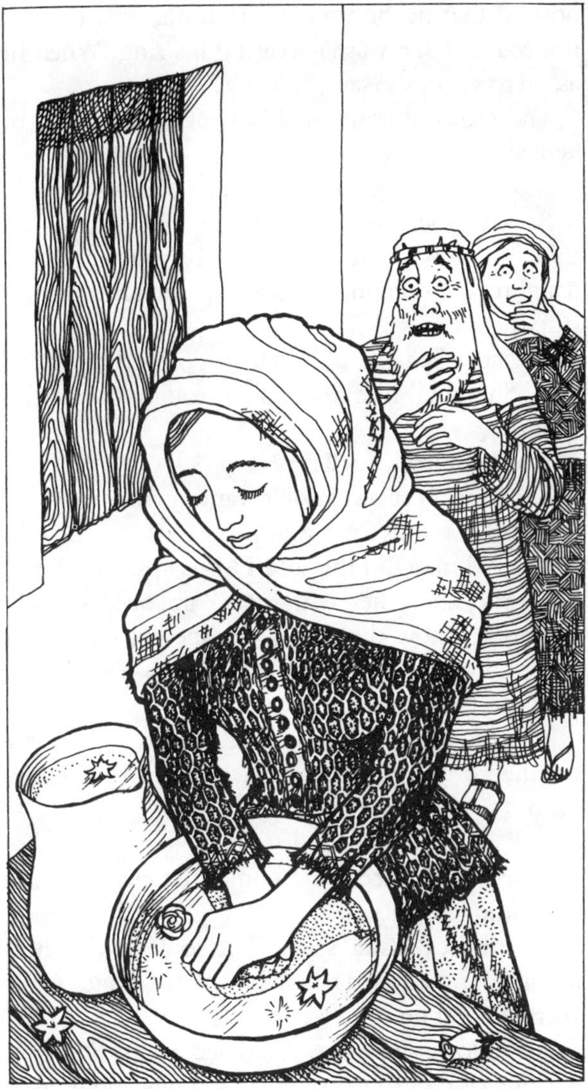

noticed that no flowers fell from her lips. He also noticed that she wasn't wearing his ring. When he asked to see it, she said, "I lost it."

The prince was worried but for the moment he kept silent.

Back at the poor man's house, Flowerlips was thinking about the prince. "My aunt and her daughter are cheating the prince," she said. "I must stop them."

So she asked the old man to go to the prince's city. She told him to walk through the streets shouting:

"I sell jasmines, I sell roses.
I don't want silver, I don't want money,
I need two eyes for my lady."

The old man did this and Flowerlips' aunt heard him. She knew her daughter Zara needed some flowers to show the prince. So she cut out Zara's eyes and gave them to the old man to pay him for the flowers.

The old man took the eyes to Flowerlips. He watched in wonder as she placed them back in her head.

When the prince came home that evening Zara was hiding her face.

"I am sick," she said, "but look at all these jasmines and roses. They fell from my mouth while you were out hunting."

And Flowerlips? She could see again. She gave her fine clothes to the old man's family and dressed in the clothes of a young boy. Then she said goodbye to the old man and his family and hurried to the prince's city.

When she arrived, she went to the palace gardens. The head gardener gave her a job there. Every day she worked hard, cutting the grass and watering the flowers. There were many beautiful flowers in the prince's garden but none were as lovely as her own jasmines and roses.

One night, when everyone was sleeping, Flowerlips ran quietly to the palace lake. She took the boy's clothes off her back and the ring off her finger. Then she began to wash herself.

That night the prince couldn't sleep. He was very worried. His mind was full of questions about Zara. He needed to clear his mind, so he decided to take a walk in the gardens.

The prince always enjoyed walking in the palace gardens. He liked all the flowers there, but he loved the jasmines and roses most of all. Tonight the smell of flowers was very strong.

As he was walking by the lake, he noticed there was something shining on a stone. He picked it up – it was Flowerlips' ring.

"It is the ring that I gave to Flowerlips," he thought with happiness.

Then he looked across the lake and saw her! Flowerlips was standing in the water shining in silver light. Her beauty was bright and lovely like the full moon that lit her. As she washed herself she sang, and the jasmines and roses fell into the water.

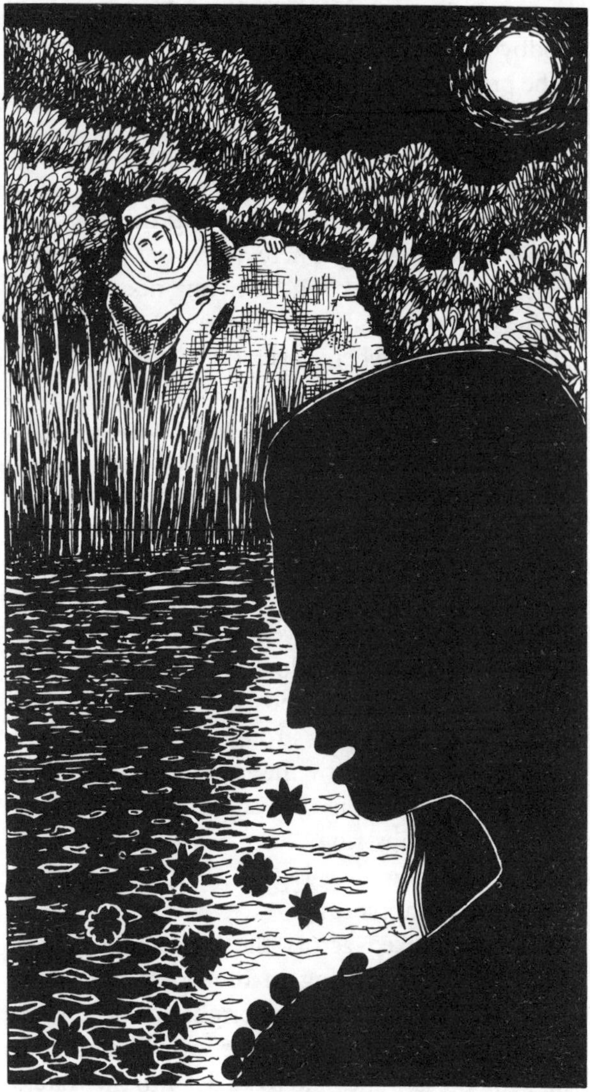

The girl finished washing and came out of the water to dress. The prince quickly hid behind a tree.

Flowerlips dressed and then bent to pick up her ring from the stone. When she discovered it wasn't there, she was very worried. She looked everywhere for it. "I'm sure I put it here on this stone," she said.

The girl was beginning to cry over her lost ring, when the prince jumped out from his hiding-place. "Here is your ring. But first tell me, who are you? I want to hear your story."

So the prince found the girl he wanted to marry. He sent the aunt and her daughter Zara back to their own city. Then he held a marriage feast that lasted forty days and forty nights.

# *The Little Red Fish and the Shoe of Gold*

There was once a fisherman who lived in an old house by a wide river. His wife was dead. She fell into the great river and left him a pretty young daughter. The little girl was only two years old and the fisherman loved her very much. Her name was Sharifa.

In a house nearby there lived a woman called Minah and her daughter. This woman's husband was also dead. He too died in the river.

Minah wanted to marry the fisherman. She began to visit his house every day. She tried to please him by taking care of his daughter. She washed and combed the little girl's hair, and said to the child, "I am like a mother to you, aren't I?"

But the fisherman didn't want to marry again. He was afraid that a new wife would hate his daughter. "I love Sharifa like the flowers love the rain. If I marry another wife she won't understand my love for Sharifa. New mothers always hate their husband's children."

The years passed and Sharifa grew more and more lovely. One day she saw her father washing his own clothes. Then she began to think, "One day I will marry and leave home. Then father will be alone. He'll be sad and lonely without me."

She felt sorry for her father, so she said, "Why don't you marry our neighbour? She is a good woman and she loves me like a daughter."

The fisherman wanted to please Sharifa, so he married his neighbour Minah, and the new wife came to live in his house.

The weeks passed and as sure as the sun rises, the new wife began to hate Sharifa. She saw that the fisherman's daughter was pretty and clever while her own child was ugly and unintelligent. She didn't want people to see the difference between them.

The new wife was now the manager of the house. She forced Sharifa to do all the work. All day, every day, she was ordered to cook the food, brush the floors, wash the pots and pans. The poor girl worked without a rest.

Minah refused to give her any soap to wash herself with, so Sharifa soon became dirty. While Minah and her daughter ate the finest meat, Sharifa lived off old bread. Soon she became thin and weak.

Although Sharifa was badly-fed and always tired, she still had a kind heart. She didn't want to worry her father, so she didn't tell him her troubles. "I must look after myself," she thought.

One of her jobs was to go to the river every day to carry home her father's fish. One evening, as she

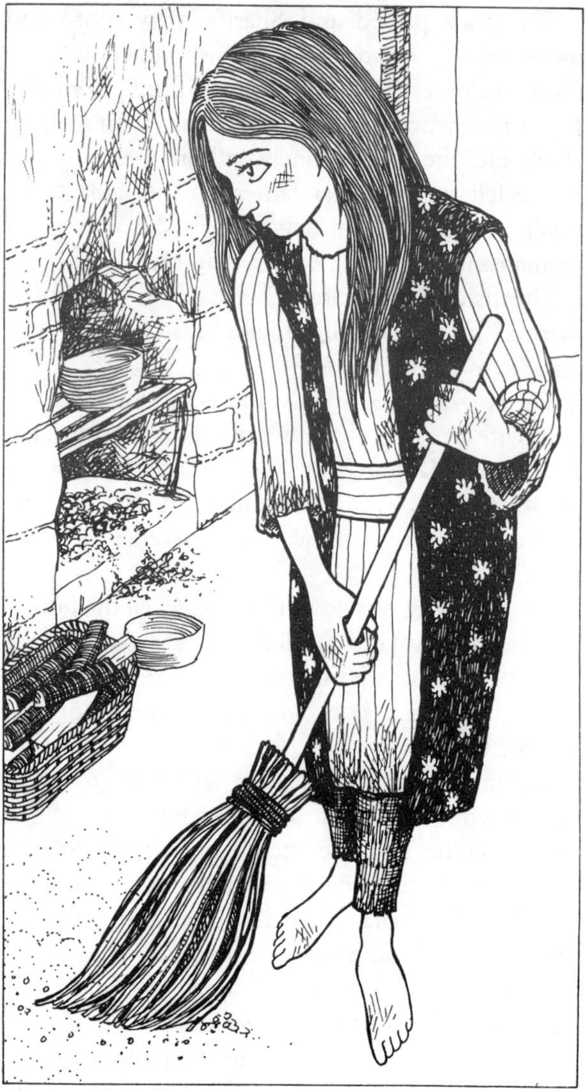

was carrying home four fish, one of them suddenly spoke to her:

"Please don't let me die.

Throw me back into the water,

And now and always be my daughter."

The girl almost dropped the bag in surprise.

"A talking fish! Is this true or are my ears cheating me?"

She stopped to listen, half in wonder, half in fear. Then she threw the little red fish back into the river. The little red fish lifted its head out of the water and said:

"Come to me when you are sad

And I will help to make you glad."

Sharifa went back to the house and gave the other three fish to Minah. When her father returned he asked about the fourth fish. She told him that she lost it on the way home.

"Don't worry," he said, "it was only a very small fish."

But Minah was angry. When the fisherman left the room she shouted at the girl, "You didn't tell me there were four fish. You didn't say that you lost one. Go back and look for it."

It was past sunset, so the girl had to walk back to the river in the dark. She stood by the river and called out to the little fish:

"Please, fish, come from the water,

So that you may help your daughter."

In a moment the fish appeared at her feet. It held a gold coin in its mouth. Sharifa bent down and took the coin.

"Take this to Minah," said the fish, "and she will not be angry."

The girl hurried home and gave the coin to Minah. The woman was very surprised and she soon forgot about the lost fish.

The years came and the years went. The two little girls became young women. Sharifa grew more and more lovely while Minah's daughter was still ugly.

One day all the women were very excited. The daughter of the richest man in the town was going to get married. On the night before the wedding, the girl was holding a party. She asked all the women to go to her home to sing, and help her paint her hands and feet. It was going to be a wonderful party. Every mother would bring her unmarried daughter to show to the mothers of unmarried sons.

"Perhaps I will find a rich husband for my daughter," thought the fisherman's wife.

Minah carefully washed her daughter and dressed her in her finest clothes. Then the two women hurried off to the party. As she left, she called to Sharifa, who was working in the kitchen as usual:

"Make sure you wash the floor well. Don't stop working until everything is clean."

Sharifa couldn't go to the party because she had no fine clothes to wear. She owned only one dress, and that was old and dirty. As she worked her heart was filled with sadness. Then she remembered the little red fish.

"It was so many years ago, but maybe it can still

help me," she said.

She ran down to the river and called for the fish. It appeared in a second.

"You shall go to the party. Here take this." The fish gave her a bag and then swam away again.

The girl slowly opened the bag and looked inside. She couldn't believe her eyes. There was a dress of the finest blue cloth, a comb of jewels for her hair and – most beautiful of all – two golden shoes for her feet.

Sharifa washed herself and put on the lovely dress. From it came the smell of roses. She placed the comb of jewels in her hair. Then she put on the golden shoes and hurried away to the party.

When Sharifa entered the room everyone became silent. They all stopped talking and turned to stare at her. "How beautiful she is," they thought, "and what lovely clothes she has. She must be the daughter of a very rich family."

Sharifa was led to a soft red seat in the middle of the room. Then the women brought her silver plates full of sweets and tasty cakes. Sharifa noticed Minah and her daughter. They were sitting near the door with the other fishermen's wives.

Minah stared at her. "That lady looks like Sharifa, but of course it cannot be her. Sharifa is at home cleaning the house," she said to herself.

Before Minah and her daughter left, Sharifa thanked her hostess and hurried out. The sun was setting and darkness was coming.

On her way home, the girl had to cross a bridge over a little river. This same stream also ran through the king's garden. As she ran over the bridge, one of the golden shoes fell into the water. She tried to reach it, but the water was too deep. So she took off the other shoe and ran home.

Ten minutes later, Minah and her daughter arrived home. They found Sharifa in her old dress, brushing the floor.

And what about the golden shoe? By chance, the water carried it down the river and into the king's garden. It came to rest at the bottom of a little lake, where the king's son brought his horse to drink.

The next morning, the prince noticed something shining at the bottom of the lake. He reached into the water and pulled out the shoe. When he held the lovely little thing, his heart was moved with love for the owner. He carried it gently back to the palace and went to find the queen.

"Mother, I want to get married."

The queen was a bit surprised. "This is very sudden, my dear. But tell me, which girl has stolen your heart?"

"That's the problem," answered the prince. "I don't know her name. I don't know where she lives or who she is. I want to marry the girl whose little foot sits inside this shoe."

The queen promised to find the owner of the shoe. The next day she began her search. She visited all the important families in the town. Every young woman she met tried on the shoe, but it didn't fit them. Their feet were much too big.

That evening, the prince asked his mother, "Did you find her?"

"Not today, son, but wait a little longer. I will find her."

She continued her search the next day. In one door and out the other, but she didn't have any luck. She didn't find the owner of the little golden shoe.

When she returned to the palace that day, the prince questioned her again.

"I'm sorry son, but I can't find the girl. I've visited all the houses but with no luck."

"What about the fishermen's homes by the river? Have you been there?" asked the prince.

"The fishermen's homes! The owner of such a valuable shoe can't be a fisherman's daughter," said the queen.

But the prince asked again and again, and in the end the queen agreed to search the fishermen's homes.

When Minah learnt that the queen was coming, she got busy. She dressed her daughter in her best clothes. She painted her eyes and combed her hair. But when she stood beside the fisherman's daughter, she was like a match beside the sun. So the stepmother pushed Sharifa into the kitchen and shut the door.

When the queen appeared at the door, Minah pushed her daughter forward. At that moment, a blue bird flew into the garden and sang:

"Ki-ki-ki-kow
Let the king's wife know,
They put the ugly one on show

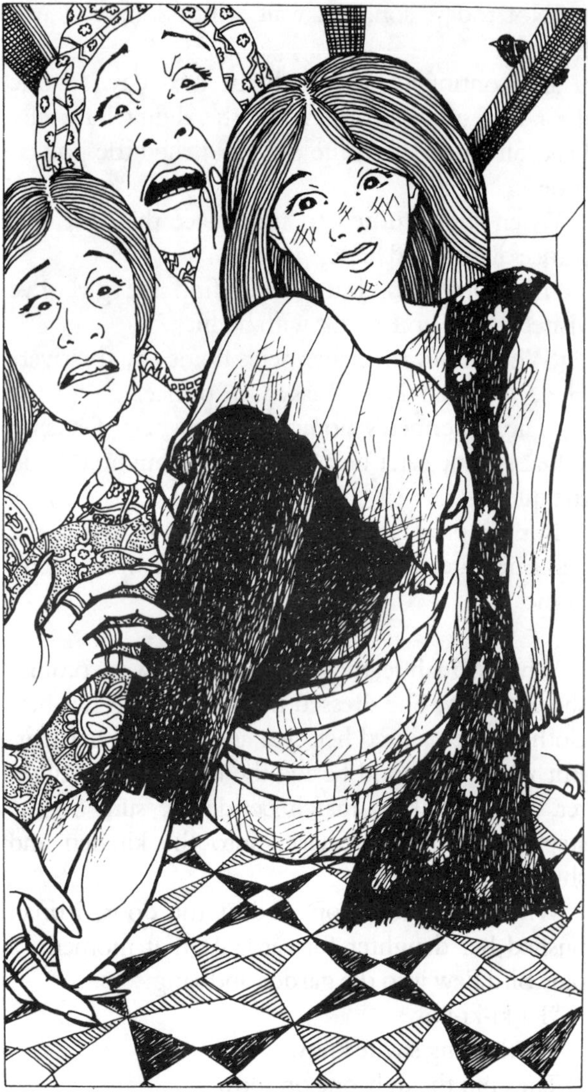

And hid the beauty down below."

The queen heard the bird and began to search the house. She looked everywhere, upstairs and down. In the end she went down to the kitchen and there was Sharifa, covered in dirt.

The girl tried on the golden shoe. Of course it fitted her little foot. The queen was very pleased. "At last I have found a wife for my son."

So the fisherman's daughter married the prince. They loved each other and were very happy together.

And Minah? After the queen left for the palace with Sharifa, she ran out of the house pulling at her hair in anger. She wasn't looking in front of her and she fell into the river. She couldn't swim, so she died.

The fisherman was once again without a wife, so he went to live with his daughter at the palace. Minah's daughter was now all alone in the world. Sharifa felt sorry for her, so she let her live at the palace as well.

Without her mother to cause trouble, Minah's daughter became a good friend to Sharifa. She didn't marry, but she helped the prince and his wife to take care of their many children.

# *Si Djeha Cheats the Thieves*

One day Si Djeha was riding his fine white horse through the town. On the road he met three thieves. They were leading a thin, old donkey to the market. When they saw Si Djeha with his beautiful horse, they called out, "Si Djeha, you are a brave man. Aren't you afraid to ride such a tall animal? If you fall you will break your neck and die. Look, we have a nice small animal here."

"Yes, you're right," answered Si Djeha. "Your donkey is much safer. I will take it and you can take my horse."

"Ah, but because we have saved your life, you must also give us one hundred silver pieces," said the thieves.

Si Djeha agreed to this. He got off his horse and gave it to the thieves. Then he rode home on the old donkey. When he arrived home his mother was very angry. "Where is your beautiful white horse?" she shouted. "What can I do with such a stupid son?"

When the next market day came, Si Djeha decided to take the donkey to town. But before he went, he fastened a few gold coins under the animal's tail. As he entered the market, he met the thieves again.

"Good day to you my friends and thank you a hundred times. Because of your kindness I'm now a rich man."

The thieves looked at each other in surprise.

"We don't understand. What do you mean?" they asked.

"This donkey is very special. What do you think it drops when it lifts its tail?" asked Si Djeha.

The thieves began to laugh.

"Dung, of course. What else does a donkey drop but dung?"

"No, you are wrong. This donkey doesn't drop dung. When it lifts its tail, gold pieces fall to the ground," said Si Djeha.

The thieves didn't believe Si Djeha, so he showed them the coins under its tail. When they saw the gold pieces, the thieves bit their fingers in anger.

"Please let us have our donkey back." they said. "We will give you your horse and one hundred and fifty silver pieces."

But Si Djeha refused. Then they offered him two hundred silver pieces, but he still refused. They asked him again and again until he finally agreed to sell the donkey for three hundred pieces of silver. Then he climbed onto his fine, white horse and, with his pockets full of silver, he turned towards home. As he rode away, he called to the thieves, "Don't forget to feed it well and put your best carpets under it to catch the gold."

The first thief took the donkey home. He cut down a whole field of grass to feed the animal. Then he put the donkey in a room with his finest carpets. Pleased with himself, he went to bed to dream of mountains of gold coins.

All night the donkey ate and ate. In the morning the thief opened the door to find mountains – mountains of dung!

That morning, it was the second thief's turn to use the donkey. The first thief felt a fool, so he didn't tell his friend about his bad luck.

The second thief also fed the donkey with a whole field of grass. He also woke to find his loveliest carpets covered in dung.

The third thief did the same as the others. But when he found his living-room full of dung he shouted angrily at the others:

"You have taken all the gold and left me nothing but dung!"

"No we haven't," said the others. "The donkey gave us only dung too. Si Djeha has cheated us. Let's go to his house and attack him."

Now Si Djeha knew the three men would come, so he made a plan. He bought three chickens and a bowl of couscous. He asked his wife to cook a tasty meal with them. When the food was ready, he put it in a pot and covered it with a plate. Then he dug a hole in the floor of the dining-room and put the food into the ground.

At midday the three thieves arrived at Si Djeha's house.

37

"Hello my friends. What a nice surprise," said Si Djeha. "But why didn't you tell me you were coming? My cupboards are empty. I haven't prepared any food. But I needn't worry because I have my special stick."

"Your special stick. What's that?" asked the thieves.

It's a very useful thing. Every good host needs one. Come in and I'll show you."

The men forgot to attack Si Djeha and followed him into the house. As they entered, Si Djeha picked up an old piece of wood from the garden. The thieves sat down and stared in surprise. Si Djeha touched the floor with the stick and then began to dig. Their faces lit up when they smelt the meal he uncovered from the floor.

"When I'm surprised by visitors," Si Djeha explained, "I don't worry because I have my special stick. With this stick I can always be a good host."

The men ate their fill, then the first thief spoke. "We would like to buy this stick. We will give you one hundred silver pieces for it."

"It's not for sale," answered Si Djeha. But the thieves asked again and again. They offered more and more money, until at last Si Djeha accepted two hundred silver pieces for the stick.

The first thief took the stick home. His wife's brother came for dinner that evening.

"Welcome dear brother," said the thief, "tonight I have a wonderful surprise for you."

Then he touched the floor with the stick and started to dig. He dug and dug until he had a great big hole in the centre of his floor but, of course, he didn't find any food. All this time his visitor was staring at him.

"My sister's husband has lost his brains," he thought. "Perhaps he is looking for them in the ground."

After an hour the visitor went home hungry. The thief didn't want his friends to laugh at him, so he didn't tell them.

The next day it was the second thief's turn to use the stick. He invited six neighbours for dinner. They watched as he dug up his dining-room floor and then returned home laughing.

"What a fool our neighbour is," they said.

The next evening the third thief invited some villagers to lunch. He too touched the floor with the stick, then started to dig. After an hour he realised that there was no food, and his visitors went home hungry.

The next day the thieves met each other at the market. "Si Djeha has cheated us again," they said angrily. "This time he will not escape us." But once again Si Djeha was ready for them.

The next morning he said to his wife, "I am going to work in the fields. If those three men come here again, send them to the east field. Then go to the shops and buy a kilo of lamb. Cook it in butter for our lunch."

Before he left, he picked up a brown bag from the garden. There was a bird inside the bag. He carried the bird to the fields with him.

Soon afterwards the three thieves arrived at Si Djeha's house. When they saw Si Djeha in the fields they called, "Hey Si Djeha! Come here. We want to talk to you."

"Okay," said Si Djeha, "but first let me send word to my wife that we're coming."

Then he pulled the bird from the brown bag. "Fly home and tell my wife to cook a meal of our best meat for our three important visitors." The bird flew away and the four men walked back to Si Djeha's house.

When they stepped into the house, they found Si Djeha's wife waiting for them. She had prepared lamb and vegetables, bowls of rice, plates of tasty sweets and fruits. There was even a large pot of rose-water to wash themselves with. Again Si Djeha was an excellent host.

When the dinner was finished, Si Djeha went outside and caught a bird in the garden. This bird was the same size and colour as the first. He took it inside.

"This bird is my little helper," he said to the thieves. "I have neither son nor daughter, but this bird does the work of many."

The thieves looked at the bird. Then the first one spoke: "Si Djeha, I need a bird like this. I want to buy it from you. How much will you sell it for?"

At first Si Djeha refused to sell the bird. He let the thieves ask again and again. In the end he agreed to sell it for two hundred silver pieces.

On their way home, the thieves decided to try out their new worker. They sent the bird to the second thief's home.

"Hurry home, bird. Tell my wife that we are coming. Tell her to cook fish and rice for our dinner," he commanded.

But when they arrived home, they saw that nothing was ready. The cooking fire wasn't even lit.

"Why haven't you cooked our dinner?" the thief asked his wife. "Didn't my new worker tell you that we were coming?"

"What worker?" asked his wife in surprise.

When they heard this, the three men turned around angrily. They hurried back to Si Djeha's house with hate in their eyes and murder in their hearts.

But before they reached Si Djeha's door, a fearful sight met their eyes. Si Djeha was shouting angrily at his wife. He held a knife in one hand. Then as they watched, the woman fell to the ground screaming. Her dress was covered in blood. Then Si Djeha touched his wife with the knife and she stood up. "Bring coffee for our visitors," he ordered. When she left the room, the thieves questioned Si Djeha.

"Have you not heard of the knife that kills and brings back to life?" he answered. "Every man with a difficult wife needs one."

Before they finished drinking the coffee, the thieves managed to buy the knife for two hundred silver pieces.

Each thief in turn used it in his home. Then, after the murder of their wives, all three thieves were put into prison for life. They didn't cause any more trouble for Si Djeha.

# *God will Help*

There was once a man called Said who lived in a small town in the south of the country. Said was neither rich nor poor. He didn't have gold, jewels and fine clothes, but his family always ate well.

Said owned a small garden. Nothing grew in his garden except one tall orange tree. This tree was the wonder of the town because it grew the sweetest oranges ever tasted.

Every morning, Said got up early and picked all the tasty oranges from the tree. Then he put them into bags and took them to the market on his donkey.

At the market he sold his fruit. Everyone loved Said's oranges. People travelled from faraway towns to buy them. So, by midday, everything was sold and he had enough money to buy meat, rice and sugar. Then he went home and spent the afternoons talking to his children.

The years passed happily. Day in, day out, nothing changed. Fat, bright oranges always appeared on the tree and Said always made enough

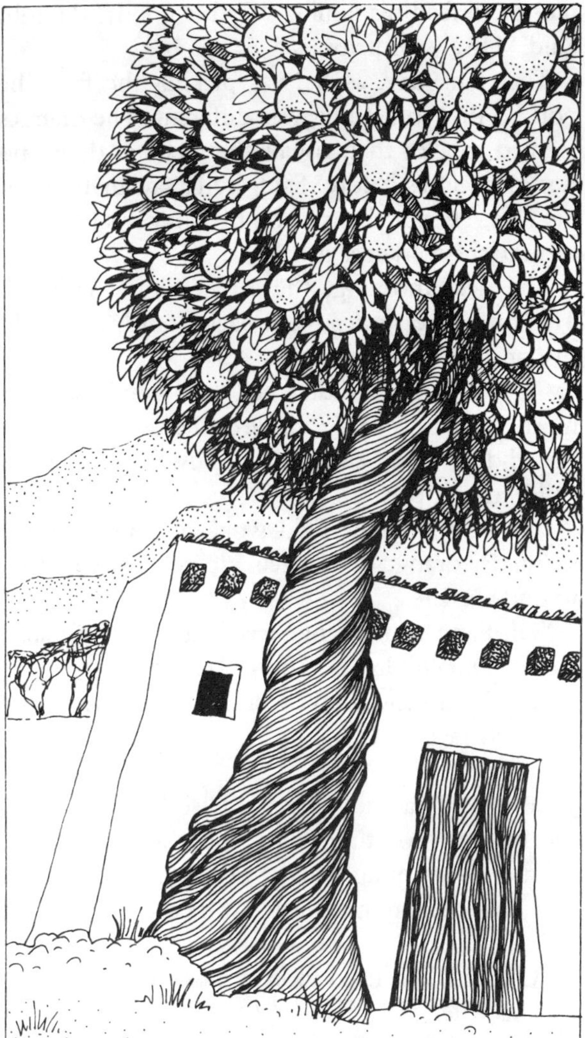

money to feed his family. "God is good," thought Said, "He always helps us."

Then one day, as he was picking the fruit, he noticed that something was different. The oranges seemed smaller than usual; they looked drier and not as sweet as before. Said didn't say anything to his wife. He put the fruit on his donkey's back and went to the market as usual.

The next morning, the same thing happened. This time Said noticed that each branch only held five or six small, dry oranges.

Once again he didn't tell his wife, and that morning he only made a little money at the market. He didn't have enough to buy meat for his children's supper.

On the third day, Said woke to find only one small, dry orange on his tree. He ran to the kitchen to find his wife.

"Oh Fatma, the orange tree is dying. What shall we do? Our children will have no food."

"Hush husband, don't worry. God will help us," said his wife quietly.

Now Said had nothing to sell, so he didn't go to the market. For three days and three nights his children went hungry and Said's heart grew heavy with sadness. On the fourth day he decided to go to the city.

"Our children need food. I must find a job," he told his wife.

So he put a blanket and a bottle of water into a bag and began to walk to the city. He walked and walked for many hours, until he met a farmer watering his fields.

"Good day, farmer. I'm looking for a job. Do you need a worker to help on your farm?"

"I'm sorry," answered the farmer, "but I have six sons. They are all the workers I need."

So Said walked on. It was midday now and very hot, but he didn't stop. He followed the dusty road for many more kilometres. After several hours he met a man making bread.

"Good evening, friend," said Said. "I am searching for a job. You seem a busy man. Perhaps you need a worker to help you?"

"I'm sorry," answered the baker, "but I have six daughters. They make all the bread and cakes I need."

Said continued walking for many more hours without meeting anyone. By now the sun was going down and it was getting dark. Said was very tired and needed to sleep. He was far from any town so he looked around for somewhere comfortable to spend the night.

He saw a large hole in the rocks, which was as big as a room. He went inside and lay down on his blanket. The moon was high in the sky, round and bright like a silver coin. It shone down on the land, lighting up the rocks, the trees and the road.

Then he noticed that he wasn't completely alone. There was a bird sitting beside the entrance. Said saw that the bird couldn't see – it had no eyes.

Said moved closer to get a better look. The bird didn't move. It remained sitting on the rock with its mouth open. Then Said noticed that its mouth was full of flies. They flew into the bird's mouth. The bird waited until its mouth was full and then ate them.

For a long time Said watched the bird in silence. Then an idea came to him.

"God helps this bird, so I am sure God will also help me."

The next day, instead of continuing his search for work, Said took the long, dusty road home. When he arrived, he lay down on his bed and went to sleep. When his wife came into the room at midday, Said refused to move.

"God will help," he said, and went back to sleep.

An hour later his wife heard someone at the door. She opened it and found two rough-looking men.

"Have you got a donkey?" they asked. "We need one to carry some vegetables to the market. We will pay you for it."

The wife agreed to let them have the donkey for a few hours and the men gave her some money.

The men led the donkey up to the mountains where they were hiding some treasure. Two days before, the men found the treasure together, but now each man was going to his own village. They had to put the treasure into two bags, one bag for the first man and one bag for the other. The first man counted out the money.

"One gold coin for you and one for me. Two silver pieces for you and two for me."

There was a lot of treasure, but after two hours it

was all in the two bags. All except a beautiful golden cup.

Now there was a problem. There was only one golden cup and each man wanted it.

"It's mine," shouted the first man seizing the cup.

"No, it's mine," cried the second man, "I saw it first," and he pulled the cup from the first man.

They began to argue, then to fight. First they pushed and hit. Then they pulled out their knives and cut each other until they both lay dead.

The donkey left the mountains and took the road home. Said's wife was very surprised to see the animal return alone. She called her husband, who was still lying in bed. Said got up and helped her to pull the animal inside.

When he opened the two bags he couldn't believe his eyes. He emptied the bags onto the bed and looked in wonder as the treasure shone in the sunlight. Then he took a handful of coins and ran to the market to buy food. His family never went to bed hungry again.

# How Si Djeha Found a Good Meal

One day Si Djeha was travelling across a wide desert. He was going to visit his uncle who lived many kilometres away. He was carrying three bags of food and drink.

On the first day he opened one of the bags. Inside there was a chicken and a bottle of water. He drank the water, ate the chicken and then went to sleep.

The next day he walked for many more kilometres. As the sun was going down, he sat down beside a rock and opened the second bag. This time he took out a bottle of water and a piece of beef. He quickly ate his supper and then went to sleep.

On the third evening he opened the third bag. This time there was a bottle of water to drink, but only a small piece of old bread to eat.

"I shan't worry," thought Si Djeha, "tomorrow I will reach my uncle's home and then I'll eat like a king."

But the fourth day came and went without any

sight of a town or village. That evening Si Djeha went to sleep hungry and thirsty.

On the fifth day he walked for many hours. His tongue felt like sand, and his legs were as weak as a new-born camel.

"I must eat and drink soon or I will die," thought Si Djeha sadly.

Then at last he saw another traveller. The man was sitting in the shade of a rock eating his midday meal. As Si Djeha came closer a wonderful smell of meat and couscous reached his nose.

"Soon I will eat," thought Si Djeha happily.

Si Djeha sat down beside the man.

"Where do you come from?" asked the man.

"From your own village," answered Si Djeha.

"May your news be good news, brother," said the man.

"And so it is," said Si Djeha.

"Tell me about my wife, Umm Othman."

"She is in very good health," replied Si Djeha.

"And Othman, my son?"

"He is still the best-looking young man in the village."

"And my camel?" asked the traveller.

"It's the fattest animal I've ever seen," replied Si Djeha.

"And my dog?"

"It watches over your house like a lion."

"And my house?"

"Like the king's palace."

Pleased with this news, the man silently returned to his meal. Si Djeha waited hopefully, but the man

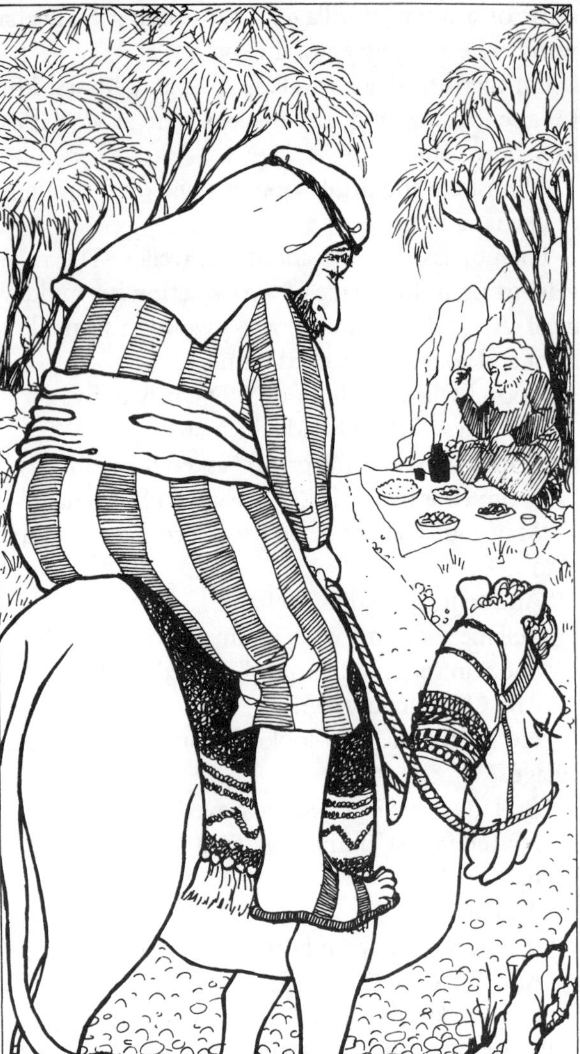

didn't offer him any food. Then suddenly Si Djeha jumped up.

"Where are you going in such a hurry?" asked the man.

"I must return to my village. Since your dog died the thieves have caused trouble."

"My dog is dead?"

"Yes."

"How did he die?"

"I think he ate too much of your camel."

"My camel is dead?"

"Yes."

"How did it die?"

"It fell over Umm Othman's body."

"My wife is dead?"

"Yes."

"How did she die?"

"Of a broken heart over Othman's death."

"My son is dead?"

"Yes."

"How did he die?"

"He was killed when the house fell on top of him."

When he heard this the man began to scream and pull at his hair. Then he ran off to the village as fast as he could.

Si Djeha reached out his right hand and started eating his dinner.

# *How the Animals Kept the Lions Away*

There was once a donkey, a horse, a dog and a chicken who had no owners. Each animal was alone in the world, so they decided to live together. They promised to be brothers and always take care of each other.

Together they walked across the desert until they reached some trees. Here there was water to drink, and shade from the hot sun. They decided to make it their home.

For many weeks everything went well. The animals were very happy together. Then one evening, after a big meal, the donkey started to sing. Now, as you know, when a donkey sings, the whole world can hear him.

"Ssh," said the other animals, "stop making that noise. A lion will hear you and then we'll all be in trouble."

But the donkey was feeling very pleased with himself and he wanted to sing. Before the others could stop him he ran away, singing noisily.

Sure enough, a hungry lion heard him and came

looking for his dinner.

"Mmm," said the lion, "a nice fat donkey. You'll make a tasty meal."

The donkey couldn't run away. He had to think of another way of escape, so he said, "Good evening lion. I will be pleased to be your dinner but one thing worries me."

"What's that?" asked the lion.

"I promised my brothers, the dog, the chicken and the horse to die with them. You must eat them as well."

The lion liked this idea, so he followed the donkey back to the others.

The other animals saw the lion coming and put their heads together to make a plan. When the lion came nearer they said, "Welcome uncle lion."

Then they all attacked and killed him. The dog ate the lion's meat, but the others kept his skin. They made it into a soft carpet for their tent.

They lived in peace for another month. Then the donkey wanted to sing again. The animals tried to stop him, but they couldn't. Once again, the donkey ran singing into the night.

A second lion hurried towards the animals. When they saw him coming they made another plan.

"Welcome uncle lion," they said, "you are a hundred times welcome. Bring a carpet, dog. We want our visitor to be comfortable."

The dog ran into the tent and brought out the lion skin.

"No, no, dog," said the chicken. "This carpet is

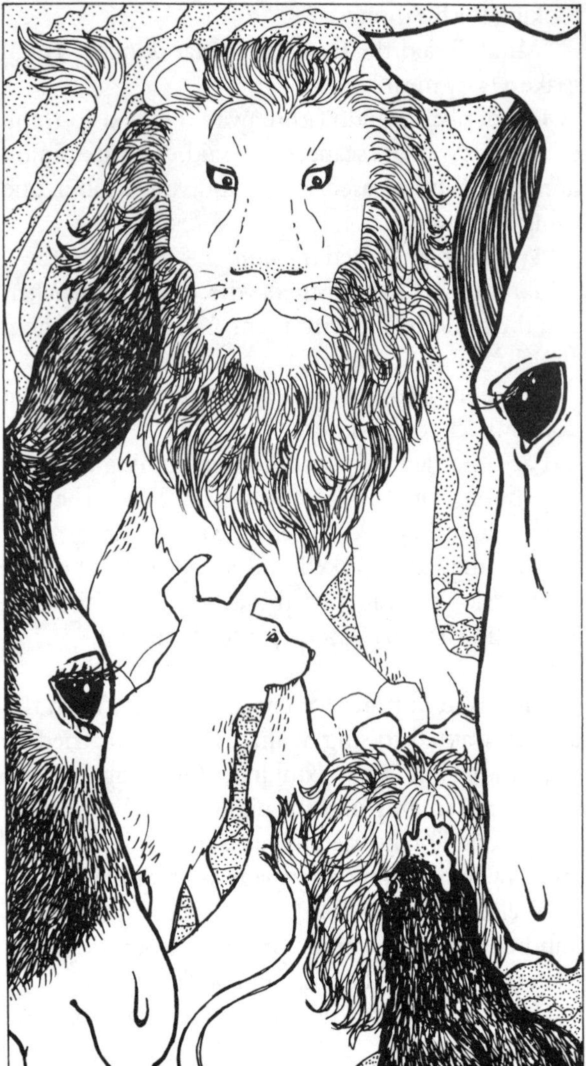

not good enough for our visitor. Bring another."

The dog carried the lion skin back into the tent. Then he brought it out a second time.

"The lion must have a softer carpet than this. Take this one back." said the donkey.

The dog took the carpet away. Then he brought it out a third time.

"This carpet is too old," said the horse, "bring a new one for our visitor."

The lion didn't wait to see. He jumped up onto his four feet and raced away as fast as he could.

The donkey still sometimes sang, but the lions never came near the animals again.

# *The Farmer Without a Brain*

Two farmers were walking through a wood to their fields when they saw the mark of a lion.

"Look, a lion has come this way. What shall we do?" said one man.

"Let's continue. We have work to do," answered the other.

So the men continued along the road. They worked all day in their fields then it was time to return.

"Let's take a different way home," said the first farmer.

"No, I'm going this way, it's shorter," answered the second man.

"Well, I'm certainly not," said the other, "I don't want to be a lion's dinner." And he took another road higher up the mountain.

The other man returned along the road through the wood. When he reached the place of the lion's mark he found the lion.

"Good evening lion," said the man.

"Good evening man," answered the lion.

"What are you doing here?" asked the man.

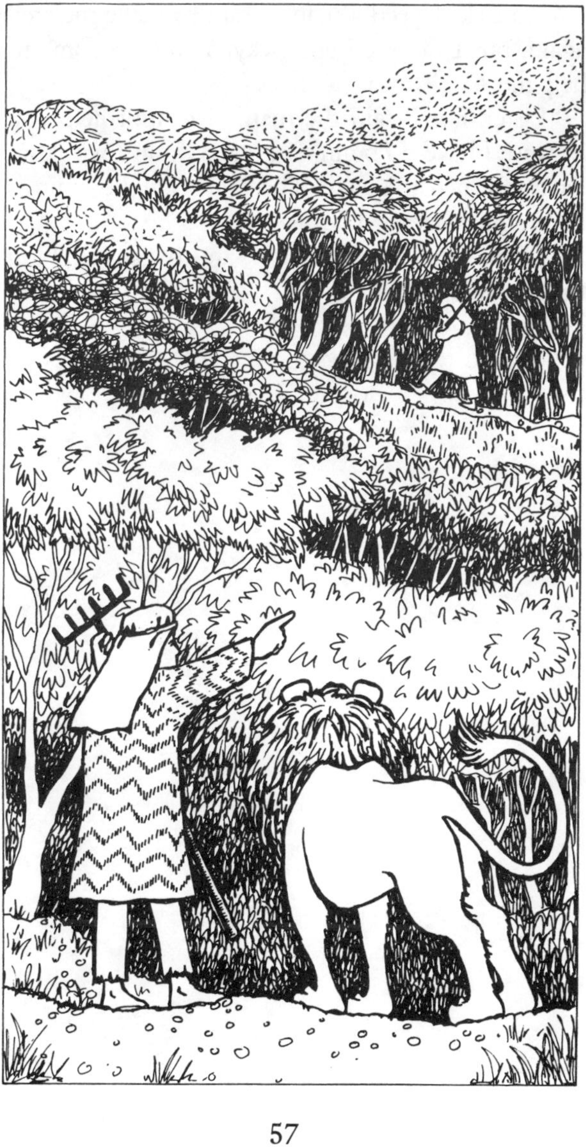

"I'm sick. I need a man's brain to make me well again, but I can see I am lucky. You have come to help me."

"Listen lion," said the man, "I cannot help you because I have no brain. If I had a brain I wouldn't have returned this way. The one with the brain is up on the other road."

"Thank you," said the lion, and began climbing the mountain.

# Crossword

## Across

2. The king's wife and the prince's mother (5)
4. When Flowerlips spoke, ........ and roses fell from her lips (8)
7. What Minah felt for Sharifa (the opposite of love) (4)
8. Everything that .......... touched turned to gold (10)
10. Sheik Hamed and Ali rode on the back of this animal (5)
11. Flowerlips cried for water because she was ....... (7)

12 I am, you are, he/she .. (2)
14 The name of the girl Ali wanted to marry (5)
15 The farmer told the lion that he did not have one of these (5)
20 The talking fish gave this to Sharifa for her hair (4)
21 Si Djeha dug it up with his stick (4)
23 The midday meal (5)
24 Flowerlips was crying for this in the desert (5)
25 The marriage feast for Flowerlips lasted ..... days and nights (5)
26 These three men stole Si Djeha's horse (7)

*Down*

1 A large area with nothing but sand (6)
3 Flowerlips lost both of these so she couldn't see (3)
4 Asila and the prince each had a ring covered with beautiful ...... (6)
5 The name of the fisherman's daughter (7)
6 Si Djeha dug up his floor with this (5)
8 Sharifa was surprised to hear this speak (4)
9 The three thieves were put in here for the murder of their wives (6)
13 The lion met one of these and ate the brain of the other (6)
16 Jasmines and ..... fell from her lips (5)
17 When you are not well, you feel ... (3)
18 The past of 'see' (3)
19 Si Djeha pretended to kill his wife with this (5)
22 The prince saw Flowerlips washing herself in this (4)

## Answers

*Across*

2 queen  4 jasmines  7 hate  8 Flowerlips  10 camel  11 thirsty  12 is  14 Asila  15 brain  20 comb  21 meal  23 lunch  24 water  25 forty  26 thieves

*Down*

1 desert  3 eye  4 jewels  5 Sharifa  6 stick  8 fish  9 prison  13 farmer  16 roses  17 ill  18 saw  19 knife  22 lake